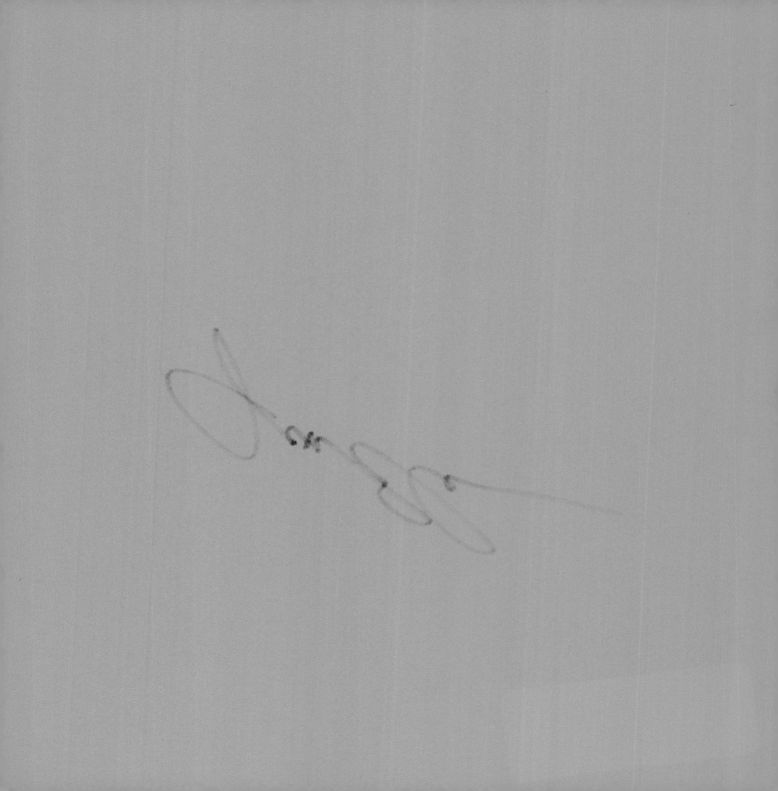

Toby's Amazing Adventures
The Great Escape

DIVINE PURPOSE PUBLISHING KIDS
An imprint of DiViNE Purpose Publishing Co.
P.O. Box 471004, Kissimmee, Florida 34747

For more exciting adventures with Toby, visit: www.TobysAmazingAdventures.com

The artwork for this book was created by Grace Vanderbush
www.gracieberckes.com

Edited by Elisa Eaton
www.livingcolorsandexpressions.com

Print ISBN: 978-1-948812-08-5
ePub ISBN: 978-1-948812-09-2

Printed in the United States of America

Toby's Amazing Adventures
The Great Escape

Justin

Toby

Dayton the Cat

Toby was a curious pup.

Nothing could keep him from adventure.

A week after arriving at his new home,
Toby felt brave enough to explore.

He discovered that his new world was very big.

He just had to see it all!

As Toby began his journey into new and unexplored places, he became very interested in a scent coming from the distance.

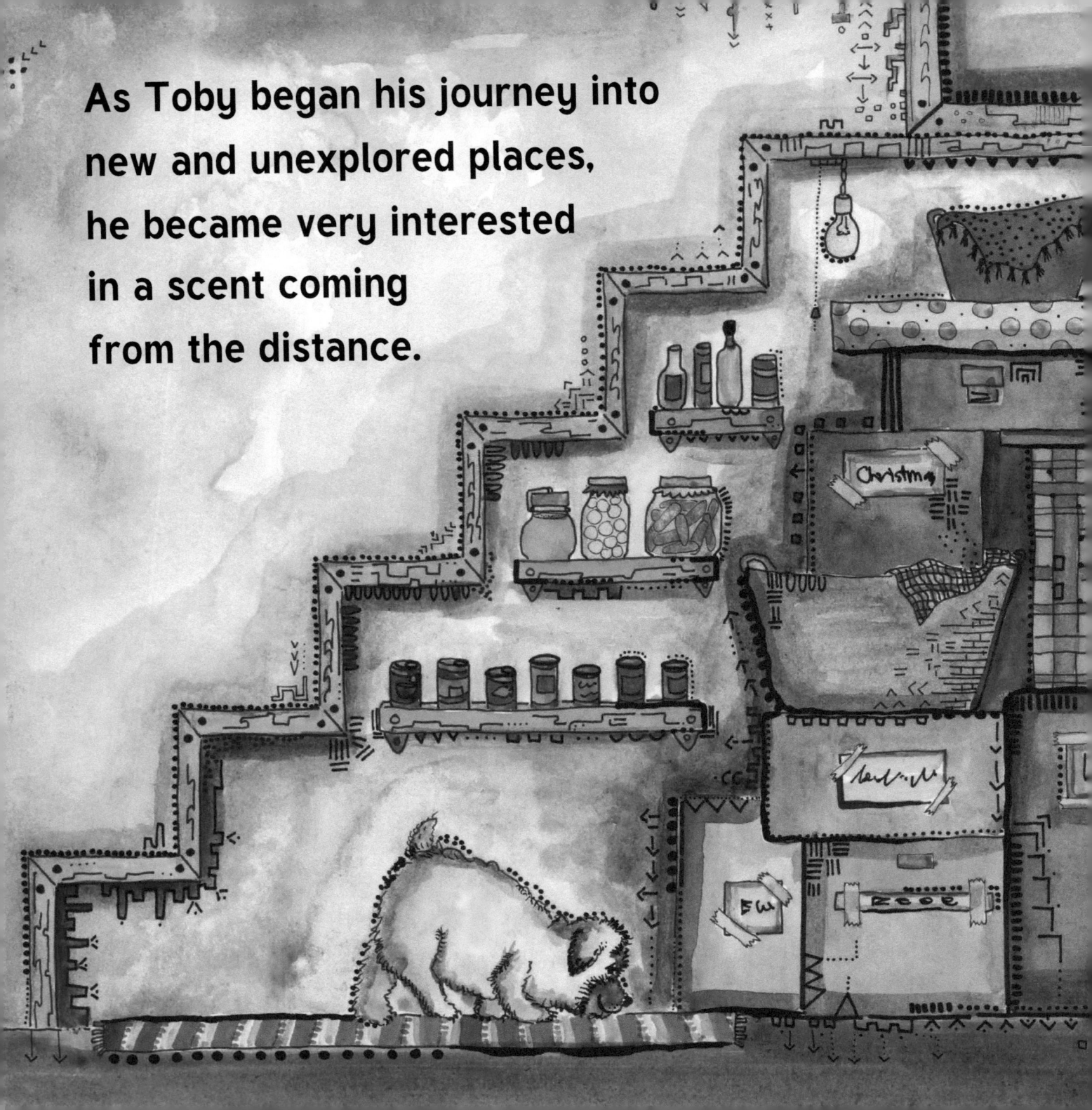

He put his nose to the ground, followed this new
scent, and wandered farther than
he had ever gone before.

As time passed and his surroundings
became less familiar, Toby discovered
that he had entered a very dark, cold cave.

"Who will save me?" Toby wondered. He had traveled so far. He was sure that no one could hear him.

Suddenly, a loud crash shook the ground
behind him. The dark cave
was now even darker.

"Oh, no!" Toby cried.

He gathered his courage and
ran back towards the entrance of
the cave to see what had happened.

Toby was surprised to find that a tall
wall of boxes had fallen
and now blocked his way.

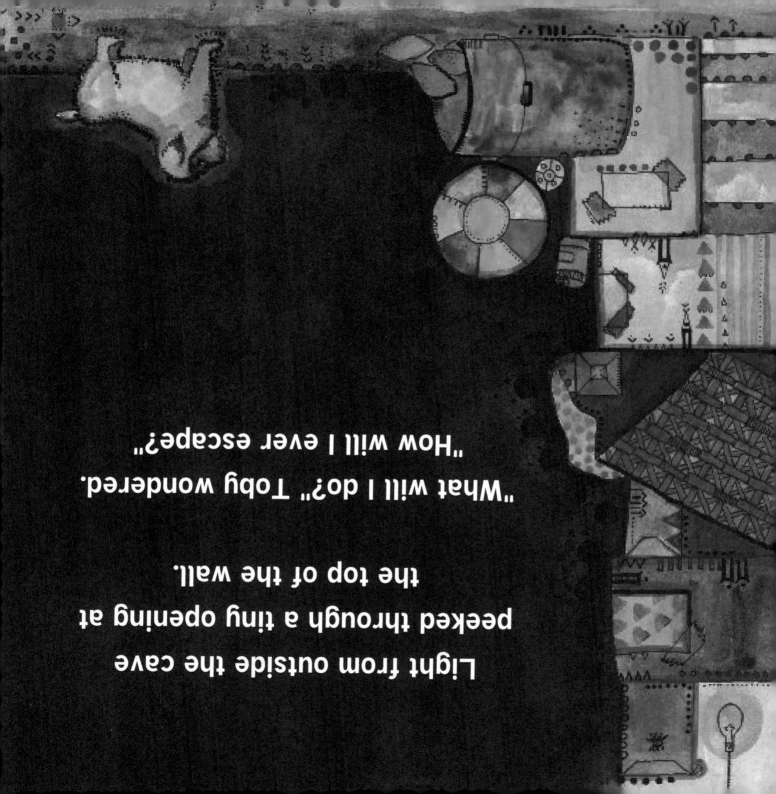

Light from outside the cave
peeked through a tiny opening at
the top of the wall.

"What will I do?" Toby wondered.
"How will I ever escape?"

Toby backed up a few steps,
took a deep breath,
and ran as fast as he could
to jump over the giant wall of boxes
blocking his way.
But the opening was too high!
He couldn't reach it!

Suddenly, he remembered what
his mother once told him.
"You are brave.
You are strong.
Never give up."

If Toby couldn't jump over the wall, maybe he could push it open. So, he put his head up against the wall of boxes and started pushing as hard as his little legs would let him.

He grunted.
He howled.
He growled.
The wall wouldn't budge!

He began to worry that he would be
trapped in this cave forever!

But Toby told himself,
"I am brave.
I am strong.
I won't give up!"

Suddenly, he noticed a set of glowing eyes staring at him from the other side of the cave. Toby was frightened by the thought of who or what was behind those scary eyes.

"Oh, I don't feel so brave right now,"
Toby said to himself.

"But I am brave.
I am strong.
I won't give up!"

So, Toby put on a brave face,
went up to the strange creature,
and barked a confident, "Hello."

A "meow" came from the direction
of the eyes that glowed in the darkness.
It was Dayton, the family cat!

Toby was so happy that
he was not alone,
and that Dayton was in
this cave with him.

"Oh, I am so glad
to see you, Dayton!"
Toby said.

Dayton jumped down from his perch and asked,
"What's wrong, Toby?"

"I'm trapped in this cave,
and I can't get out!"
Toby said.

"Never fear, young pup.
I will show you a way out,"
said the wise cat.

Dayton climbed up to the top of the wall and pushed a box to the floor to reveal more light.

The pile of boxes that had fallen
now created steps that Toby could climb up.

There was now a way for Toby
to escape to freedom!

As he reached the top of the wall in his path, his owner, Justin, called out to him in surprise. "Oh Toby, what are you doing in there?"

Justin lovingly grabbed Toby from the top of the wall and gave him a big hug.

Toby wagged his tail, and he could not stop giving Justin kisses on the cheek and mouth.

Justin smiled and said, "Oh Toby, you are quite the explorer."

Toby's adventure turned out to be quite exciting. He learned that he was a big puppy because he is strong and brave and never gives up!

CPSIA information can be obtained
at www.ICGtesting.com
Printed in the USA
BVHW022353020119
536885BV00001B/1/P